A Style All Her Own

by Laurie Friedman

illustrations by Sharon Watts

Carolrhoda Books, Inc. • Minneapolis

Carolrhoda Books, Inc.
A division of Lerner Publishing Group
241 First Avenue North
Minneapolis, MN 55401 U.S.A.

Website address: www.carolrhodabooks.com

Library of Congress Cataloging-in-Publication Data

Friedman, Laurie B.,
    A style all her own / by Laurie Friedman ; illustrations by Sharon Watts.
        p.   cm.
    Summary: Isabelle Ashley, forced to abandon her sense of style when she dresses for her cousin's wedding, finds a way to express her individuality after all.
    ISBN: 1-57505-599-6 (lib. bdg. : alk. paper)
    [1. Individuality—Fiction. 2. Clothing and dress—Fiction. 3. Weddings—Fiction.] I. Watts, Sharon, ill. II. Title.
    PZ7.F89773Sty 2005
    [E]—dc22   2004002738

JAN 0 4 2006

Manufactured in the United States of America
1 2 3 4 5 6 – JR – 10 09 08 07 06 05

For My Family—
my favorite style is when I'm with you
And with special thanks to Rebecca Ades—
your sensational sense of style sparked it all

—L.F.

For Elderine and Virginia,
because a grandmother's love
is the best sense of style
any girl can inherit

—S.W.

Isabelle Ashley Parker McBride
had a style all her own.

She had a going-to-the-grocery-store style

and a *trip-to-the-post-office* style.

She had a day-at-the-beach style

Isabelle Ashley Parker McBride had a style
all her own, and no matter where she
went, no matter what she did,
everyone said it was so.

flower shoppe

$3 DOZEN

LILACS

SEEDS

"You're in rare bloom," proclaimed Mrs. Rosebud
when Isabelle Ashley frequented her flower shop.

"You're in fine form," remarked Mr. Masterpiece when Isabelle Ashley toured the art museum.

"You're looking dishy," declared Miss Dixie when Isabelle Ashley dropped in for dinner at her diner.

Isabelle Ashley Parker McBride had a style all her own, and whenever she looked in the mirror, she'd turn and twirl and dip and dance with delight . . .

Isabelle Ashley Parker McBride liked what she saw.

One day Isabelle Ashley received an invitation
to join her Great-Aunt Savannah and
her cousin Dora for tea.

Dear Ellen, Helen, and Daisy May,
Clara, Sarah, and Samantha Kay,
Clarice, Patrice, and Martha Hannah,
Hallie, Allie, and Annabelle Anna,
Isabelle Ashley and Shelby Celeste,

The thing in this world we'd both like best
is if you'd kindly join us for high tea,
Saturday afternoon, a quarter past three.
We've an announcement of great import.
(A hint: it's of the matrimonial sort!)

Hugs & Kisses,
Aunt Savannah and Dora

As she walked to the party,
Isabelle Ashley felt as light
as the feathers on top
of her tea hat . . .

she couldn't wait
to get there.

When she arrived, she was seated at a table with all her first cousins.

She scarcely had time to make the proper hellos before Aunt Savannah began tapping her teacup with her sugar spoon to make an announcement.

"My darling Dora is getting married, and she'd like each
and every one of you to be flower girls in her wedding."

The room filled with oohs and aahs and screams and squeals
of soon-to-be flower girls, but none were as loud as Isabelle Ashley's.
She had not the least bit of trouble imagining herself as a flower girl.

Aunt Savannah continued tapping her teacup until the room was once again quiet. Then she held up one of the flower girl dresses they would all be wearing.

"It's positively perfect!" squealed Samantha Kay.

"It's petal pink!" screamed Daisy May.

"It's like a dream come true," sighed Dora, as she passed around tea and cookies and petal pink dresses.

But Isabelle Ashley was quiet. Of all the flower girl styles she had imagined, this wasn't one of them.

Isabelle Ashley Parker McBride packed her petal pink
dress in her purse and began the long walk home.

Back in her room, Isabelle Ashley tried on her dress.

She turned and twirled.

She dipped and danced.

She even pinned up her peplum.

But no matter what she did . . .
Isabelle Ashley Parker McBride didn't like what she saw.

The next morning, she picked up the phone and slowly dialed Aunt Savannah.

"I can never be the sort of flower girl Dora dreams of," Isabelle Ashley explained to Aunt Savannah.

"Nonsense," explained Aunt Savannah, who said she understood perfectly
well what might be going through a head as stylish as Isabelle Ashley's.

tiara town

She suggested they meet
for a stroll in the park
that very afternoon.

So Isabelle Ashley Parker McBride met her Great-Aunt Savannah in the park where they strolled and swung and fed the ducks. And when it was time to go, Aunt Savannah passed along to Isabelle Ashley something that had been passed along to her when she was a little girl . . . a tip from her very own Great-Aunt Fanny.

"My Great-Aunt Fanny always told me it was fine to have a style all your own, but the trick is knowing when to have it," said Aunt Savannah.

Then she tossed the remainder of the bread crumbs to the ducks and winked at Isabelle Ashley... and together they began the walk home.

And at her cousin Dora's wedding . . .

Isabelle Ashley Parker McBride dressed like all the other flower girls.

Isabelle Ashley Parker McBride walked down the aisle like all the other flower girls.

Isabelle Ashley Parker McBride
even flung flower petals and
bowed to the bride just
like all the other
flower girls.

In fact, she looked so much like all the other flower girls, it was hard to tell just which one she was. But at the reception...

Isabelle Ashley
Parker McBride
had a style all her own.